For Alexander

The Crabtree Chronicles

Best Wishes

Frankie and the Führer

Robin Kingsland

The Crabtree Chronicles

Frankie and the Führer

Hodder
Children's
Books

a division of Hodder Headline plc

Published in Great Britain in 1998
by Hodder Children's Books

A Catalogue record for this book is available from
the British Library

ISBN 0 340 69990 6

Typeset by Avon Dataset Ltd, Bidford-on-Avon, Warks
Printed and bound in Great Britain by
Mackays of Chatham, Chatham, Kent

Hodder Children's Books
A division of Hodder Headline plc
338 Euston Road
London NW1 3BH

Thanks to Marian Noble and the Children of the Robin Hood School, Sutton

This . . .

is Eddie Crabtree

Eddie is an ordinary boy, living in an
ordinary town, doing ordinary things. But
Eddie has some extraordinary ancestors.

Like Frankie.

Frankie Crabtree is Eddie's great grandmother, but back in 1941, she was an eight-year-old evacuee.

This is Frankie's story...

1

In the village hall, preparations were well under way. There was going to be a party tonight.

Not that this was anything for Frankie and Sam to get excited about – kids weren't invited.

Especially evacuee kids like them.

They'd arrived from London a few weeks before, packed off to the country to get away from the bombing. Frankie's family hadn't liked to see them go.

It's not right – letting Hitler drive our little ones away!

He's not driving us, Gran – we're going by train!

But off they'd gone, with their little name labels and their gas masks. The minute

they'd
arrived at the
tiny railway station,
they'd formed a crocodile
with all the other evacuees
and tramped along to the
village hall. Three hours
after that they'd been
billeted with the
Tanner family.

And every
day since then
they'd been on
the receiving end
of Mrs Tanner's own
special brand of hospitality.

11

Today Mrs Tanner had been particularly short-tempered. Frankie and Sam had heard her telling Mr Tanner that she needed to make things for the party. Frankie had assumed she meant fish-paste sandwiches or something. Then she'd heard Mrs Tanner ask her husband for pipe cleaners "for my spider".

"Is she talking about the spider that lives in my bedroom?" Sam had asked. "Does he eat pipe cleaners?" Mrs Tanner had heard him. She was not pleased

"If you la di da city children don't find this house clean enough," she said, with deep sarcasm, "you know what you can do!"

And that's why Frankie and Sam found themselves kicking their heels on the wall, watching the wooden tables being set up, and cups and saucers being laid out in regimental order, and strings of flags being pinned up around the high beams of the village hall. It looked warm and cosy in there, compared to the autumn chill they were sitting in.

Someone in the hall started putting up the blackout curtains.

"Come on, Shrimp," Frankie said to her little brother.

"But I want to see the band!" Sam whined. A thin spotty youth had just started manhandling a big bass drum from a van to

the open door. Sam hopped down and took a few steps nearer.

"No, Sammy!" commanded Frankie, "Wet Blanket's in there!"

Wet Blanket, alias Mr Watts-Blunkett,
was the town clerk. A small, mean man, he
disliked children in general, and evacuees in
particular. He never missed an
opportunity to tell them
off, move them on,
or bawl them out.
Frankie reckoned
the only reason he
didn't tar and
feather them
was because
tar was rationed,
there being a
war on and all.
Normally the
very mention of Wet
Blanket's name would
be enough to freeze Sam
in his tracks, but the
thought of seeing real
drums was irresistible.
Before Frankie could
grab him, Sam was at the door.

Frankie sighed and followed him.

"Look, Frankie," Sam whispered in an awestruck voice. "Ain't it smashin'?"

"Yeah, smashin'," Frankie said. "Now come on!"

Mr Watts-Blunkett had spotted them, and now the town clerk was bearing down on them. Frankie tugged her little brother's arm. He resisted. She tugged again. Sam clung like a limpet to the door jamb. Frankie tugged a third time. This time, finally, Sam let go. The two children shot back. If Harry Seymour hadn't been there, they'd have gone flat on their backsides.

When she saw Harry's face, Frankie wished they had.

Everyone in town knew Harry. Harry dressed better than anyone else. He drove a better car than anyone else – a long black thing that must have drunk petrol like an overheated sheepdog – and he seemed to have more money than anyone else. There was a simple explanation for all this.

Harry Seymour was a crook.

Because of the war, a lot of things were in short supply –

eggs,

meat,

petrol –

virtually everything – and you were only allowed to buy so much of each thing a week, using ration coupons. But some people, by hook, or usually by crook, got hold of rationed goods, and sold them for much more than they were worth.

Harry was one of the people who worked this so-called "black market". Nobody had actually caught him at it, but everybody knew he did it.

Frankie felt a strange sensation when she fell against Harry's fancy camel coat.

Instead of a soft thud, there was a funny crunchy feeling, and a muffled squelchy sound like . . . well, *exactly* like . . . breaking eggs.

Harry glared at Frankie. He took his hand slowly from his coat pocket, and watched the sloppy, yellowy, gooey gloop

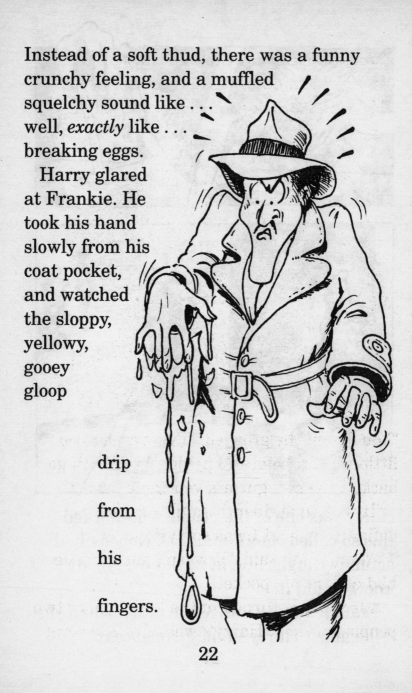

drip

from

his

fingers.

"You stupid little tyke!" he snarled.
"Sorry," Frankie said. "I couldn't help it!"
Mr Watts-Blunkett loomed behind her.

"You again!" he growled. "I've warned you
little vermin before! Why don't you both go
back to the city gutters you came from!?"

"It was an accident!" said Frankie
defiantly. "I said I was sorry!"

"Yeah," Sam said, "it wasn't our fault he
had eggs in his pocket!"

A few heads turned in the hall. One or two
people smirked. Harry's weaselly face went

red to the ears. "You little . . ."
he snarled, and raised
his hand menacingly.

Sam and Frankie
were city kids. They didn't
know much, but they knew
how to take evasive action.
They ducked under
Harry's arm
and ran.
They ran
until they
were out of
the village. They
clattered helter skelter
down the hill, and they didn't
stop until they were over the little bridge.

Frankie collapsed, gasping for breath.

"What are we going to do now, Frankie?"
asked her little brother,
as if nothing had
happened.

Frankie thought
for a minute. A watery sun
was dipping towards the hills that
flanked the village. There were farms over
there. Frankie smiled at her little brother.

25

"You want to see a pig, Sammy?" she
asked.

2

They were halfway to the farm when they were ambushed by George.

"Handy Hock!" yelled the little cockney, leaping out at them.

"That's German for 'hands up'!"

"Push off!" Frankie said. "That's English for 'kindly go away'."

Frankie always talked to George like that. He didn't seem to mind. George's skin was as thick as a tank's – just as dirty too, usually. He was a pain, but he was another evacuee, and evacuees had to stick together.

"Where you going?" he asked, falling into step with them.

"Up to the farm," Frankie said. "I was going to show Sammy a real live pig, but you've saved me a trip."

"Ha, ha."

"How about you?"

George looked all around to check that the coast was clear. "I'm going scrumping!" he whispered.

Sam immediately demanded to know what scrumping was.

"It's nicking apples," Frankie explained.

"I'm not *nicking* them," George protested. "I'm just doing my bit for the war effort by feeding the nation. Well, part of it, anyway.

You can come if you like."

"Yeah!" Sam said, enthusiastically, but Frankie, as older sister, took a strong moral stand.

"Pigs first," she declared.
"*Then* scrumping."

Frankie lifted her brother's feet onto the second rung of the gate so that his chin rested on the top. "There you are, Shrimp!" she said. "Your first pig."

Sammy looked in
disgust at the little
black and white thing
snuffling in the mud.

"That's never a pig,"
he announced.

"'Course it is."

"It's the wrong colour," Sammy said. "Pigs
is pink – 'sides, its tail's not curly-whirly."

"Maybe it's ill," said George, helpfully. Frankie dug him in the ribs.

"If it's a pig," asked Sam, "where's the slot?"

"What slot?" George asked.

"The slot for putting the money in."

"There's no slot, stupid!" George said. Frankie gave him a hard look.

"He's only four!" she said. "The only pig he's ever seen is his money box at home!"

"Here!" George said suddenly. "I'll show you something more interesting than pigs. Look!"

He pulled his fist from his shorts pocket and held it out. Unfurling his fingers with a magician's flourish, he revealed a twisted lump of muddied, rusting metal.

"What is it?" asked Sam.

"Shrapnel," George said softly.

Frankie laughed. "Geddaway!" she exclaimed. "That's a bit of tin can, that is."

"Tis not!" said George sulkily. "It's shrapnel. Not long ago that was wrapped around a hundred pounds of high explosive!"

"More like half a pound of corned beef!" Frankie said. "Where did you find it?"

"I swapped for it," said George.

"You were done!" said Frankie.

"Ah, what would you know?" said George. "You're just a girl."

Frankie would have taken up this last point, but she was distracted by the tramp, tramp, tramp of hobnails approaching.

"Hooray!" cried George with a mischievous grin. "It's Dad's Army!"

"Our dad?" asked Sammy, hopefully.

"No, Sam," said Frankie with a sigh. "Just . . . watch the pig."

Around the corner came a platoon of men in Home Guard uniform. They were a motley bunch. They wore an assortment of headgear, from cloth caps to tin helmets, and if their headgear was a mixed bag, it was nothing to their weapons. There were pitchforks and axe-handles and old service

revolvers and double-barrelled shotguns. The two youngest members of the platoon had no weapons at all, just tommy-gun shapes cut out of wood.

George spotted someone he knew – a lad who worked at the garage. "Where have you been, Jack?" George called out.

The boy shot a glance at his commander before saying, "Can't tell you. You know what they say, 'Careless talk costs lives'."

An older man next to him said, "We've been looking for Adolf. Isn't that right, Jacko?" And he winked.

George looked at Jack's wooden gun and laughed. "What were you going to do if you found him? Fill him full of splinters?"

"Cheeky beggar!" Jack said. "We're waiting for the ministry to send us guns. In the meantime, I've got this!" and from his pocket he pulled a pearl-handled penknife.

"I see," George said. "You're going to whittle him to death!"

"Eyes front!" called a gruff voice. It was the platoon commander.

"Clear off, you two," Jack said. "You're going to get me into trouble!"

Frankie and George slowed down and let the platoon march on. As they rounded the next corner, the older man called back over his shoulder.

"If you run into Adolf," he yelled, "let us know. There's a reward." And with a smoky laugh, he fell back into step and disappeared.

Silence returned. Then George cocked his head to one side. "What's that?" he asked.

Frankie listened. From way up the road, a small, plaintive four-year-old voice could be heard.

3

As soon as Sam had been rescued from the gate, the three evacuees set off on their scrumping expedition. As they did, they heard the drone of an aeroplane somewhere above.

"One of ours," George said, as if he were actual part-owner of the thing. "I can always tell."

"So can I," said Frankie. "Their's drop bombs!"

"Naaa!" George snorted. "You can tell by the engine noise. My brother taught me that. He flies bombers."

Frankie stopped. "I thought he was a commando!"

"Ah . . . that's my other brother."

Frankie frowned. To date George had about fifteen brothers, and amazingly enough, every man Jack of 'em was doing some vital war work.

They seemed to have walked miles.

"Are you sure you know where you're going?" Frankie asked. Of course, George assured her. This operation had been planned to the last detail.

"This is exactly the right time for it," he said. "It's getting dark."

"I know," Frankie said. "Misty, too. I can hardly see where I'm going. Have you got a torch?"

"No!"

"I see. I suppose it was part of your plan that we keep falling over things in the dark."

"*You* keep falling over things. I worked out the route in advance, so I wouldn't . . .

OOF!

"Don't tell me," Frankie said wryly, "somebody moved that tree."

They had reached what George called "The Target Area". A high brick wall ran as far as Frankie could see – which admittedly wasn't very far. Where George had stopped, she could just make out an old broken farm barrow propped up against a pile of wooden boxes. It had been dumped there, according to George, by the land girls that were working the farm while the labourers were off fighting.

This would be their stairway to apple heaven.

41

"It doesn't look very safe," Frankie said.

"It'll be fine," George said. "Now you keep watch."

He started gingerly edging up the barrow.

"Have you got a sack?" said Frankie.

"What for?"

"For the apples!"

"Er . . . no. I'll only pick as many as I can put in my pockets."

"Great planning. That'll be one each then . . . Not counting Sam!"

"Just keep watch, all right!"

"Yes, mon capitan!"

Frankie watched as George disappeared over the wall, then listened as he dropped down on the other side and swished off through the grass to find his ill-gotten gains. She waited. Minutes passed. Then some more minutes. Then a few more. How long can it take to find two apples. Frankie thought. Even in the dark? Sam was starting to get restless, and Frankie was just about to give up and go home, when she heard a very fast swishing from the other

42

side of the wall. There was another sound too – a harsh, rough breathing, like someone with a bad throat.

An arm appeared, followed shortly by George's head. He tried to smile.

"Get down here!" Frankie snapped.

"I can't," George hissed. "My trousers are caught!"

"What on?"

"A dog," I think.

An ominous growl confirmed this. Frankie turned to Sam. "Give us a shout if you see anyone coming," she said. She left him peering into the gloom, and stomped bad-temperedly up the barrow.

She grabbed George's arm and heaved.
There was a muffled r-r-rip! and the rest of
George came flying over the wall. For a
moment, he got a footing, but it was only a
moment.

The next thing he knew, he was flying

down the woodpile using his bottom for a
brake.

He arrived at Sam's feet with a yelp.
Frankie helped him up.

"Well?" she asked. "Where are the apples?"

"There er . . . weren't any," the boy said.
"Just the dog. I didn't think you'd want
that."

"More of your great planning?" Frankie
sighed. George rubbed his backside.

"It's not my fault," he grumbled. "I was given bad information!"

"Who by? The same kid who gave you the shrapnel?"

"Yes. How did you know?"

"Call it a lucky guess," Frankie said.

Sam tugged Frankie's arm.

"What is it, Shrimp?" she asked.

"You said to shout if someone was coming."

"Yes. So?"

So...

SOMEONE'S COMIN'!

Frankie grabbed Sam and scrambled behind the barrow. George followed them. They held their breaths and waited.

Nothing happened.
Eventually George got up and straightened his pullover.

"He must have been hearing things!" he said.

"Shhhhh!"
There was a sound coming from down the hill. A sort of "clickety-tickety" sound. Then they saw a single light wobbling in the mist.

"Blimey!" George whispered, looking at Sam. "His ears must be good!"

"Who is it?" Frankie asked.

"How should I know?" said George. "Whoever it is, they're not good on a bike!"

It was true. Now the bike was nearer, they could just about see it, wobbling and veering all over the road. They began to get an idea of the rider. He wore a cloth cap, and carried a duffle bag over his shoulder. It was the bag that was causing the trouble. Every few feet it would slide round under the cyclist's arm, and while he was elbowing it back into place, he would temporarily lose control of the bike. Then, as soon as he pulled himself back on to a straight course, the bag would slide round

again.

When the cyclist was about ten yards away from them, he clearly decided he'd had enough. Half-climbing, half-falling off the bike, he grunted something and threw the duffle bag to the ground. He wheeled the bike to the wall, propped it up, and walked back to where the duffle bag lay.

That was when he looked up.

The light from the bike lamp shone into his face. For the first time they got a good look at him. Frankie gasped.

"Look," Sam started to whisper, "it's—" but Frankie clamped a hand over his mouth. She turned to George. George's mouth was open wide. His eyes were even wider. He hardly dared to breathe.

"Is that who I *think* it is?" he managed to

say in a strangled whisper.

Frankie nodded slowly.

"*Adolf Hitler!*" she gasped.

Sam pulled a face. "That's what *I* was going to say!" he hissed.

4

There could be no mistake. They'd seen the Führer's picture all over the place. The glaring eyes, the lank hair flopping over his brow, and that unmistakable little moustache, like a fat, black exclamation mark.

Oh, it was him all right.

The Home Guard had been up looking for him. They'd said as much. They must have just missed him.

"No wonder he
can't ride a bike,"
George whispered.
"Nazis don't use 'em."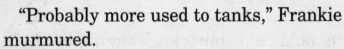

"Probably more used to tanks," Frankie
murmured.

Hitler was still messing about in his duffle
bag. He drew out a long thin object and then
shoved it back in again.

"Crikey!" Frankie gasped. "He's got a gun!"

"'Course he has. You don't think he'd come
here without one, do you?"

Suddenly Frankie pushed George's face
down. Adolf was on the move again. The
three children tried desperately to blend
into the woodpile as he clambered back on to
his bicycle and wobbled slowly up towards
the brow of the hill.

"But what would Adolf be doing here?"
Frankie gibbered, clambering out of her
hiding place.

"Yeah," Sam agreed. "There's nothing to do
here. Not even 'pictures'."

"I'll bet he came out of that plane we heard," George declared. "I knew it was one of theirs!"

"But you told me . . ."

"Yeah . . . I er . . . I didn't want to scare your kid brother," George said quickly. He ran across the road to the wall.

"Well, come on!" he said.

"Come on where?"

"If he's heading for the village," George explained. "He's got to go the road way, which means half a mile uphill before he can go downhill to the bridge. If we cut through the fields, we can beat him to it."

"And do what?"

"Tell the Home Guard, of course!"

"What! And let them get the reward? Not on your Nelly! We'll do this ourselves. We'll show 'em what evacuees are made of! Come on. We'll head him off at the bridge!"

The three children stumbled down into the chilly mist of the valley, keeping track of Adolf's slow progress by listening to the distant squeak of his bicycle wheels. By following the river, they soon found their way to a stile right next to the bridge.

SQUEAK!

SQUEAK!

Frankie could see the signpost on the other side of the road. At least, what was left of it. The Ministry of War had taken down all the pointers to confuse the Germans if they invaded. A lot of people had laughed when they'd done that. They won't be laughing tomorrow, Frankie thought with a shudder.

George was just clambering over the stile, when Frankie saw something. She dragged George back. Holding a warning finger to her lips, she pointed.

There was a car peeping out of a farm gateway. A big car. A car so black you could only see it by the gleam of the paintwork. The sort of car that could drink petrol like an overheated sheepdog. And hovering near it in the gloom was the pinpoint glow of a cigarette end.

"Harry!" George breathed.

The black-marketeer
stepped out of the shadows.

"Should we warn him? About Hitler, I mean?" Frankie asked.

But it was too late. At that moment they heard the Führer's bike. It was on the downward slope now, picking up speed as it went. Good, thought Frankie. She didn't want Harry spotting who was on it. *They*'d found Hitler and *they* were going to get the reward.

But the heroes were in for a shock. Instead of flying straight over the bridge, Hitler put on the brakes. And as he squealed to a halt, Harry stepped into the middle of the road.

Hitler propped the bike against the stile. Frankie held her breath. The leader of the Nazi war machine was just inches from them. They could have spat at him, and George was seriously tempted. Instead, he watched as Hitler walked over to Harry, and the two men began to talk in low voices.

"They know each other!" Frankie said in a shocked whisper.

"I might have guessed!" said George gravely. "Harry's a stinkin' fifth columnist."

"What's a stinkin' fib colonist?" Sam asked.

Frankie knew. People talked all the time about the fifth columnists – traitors who lived in Britain, pretended to be British and on our side, while they were actually working for the Nazis.

"Harry a traitor. That's terrible." Frankie murmured.

"No it's not, it's great!" whispered George. "I never liked him, and now there'll be two rewards! Keep watch, will you?" Without further warning he got flat down on the grass, and started to wriggle under the stile.

Harry and Hitler were still deep in conversation. Frankie couldn't hear whether they were talking in German or English, but as George reappeared, she saw the spiv hand Adolf a parcel.

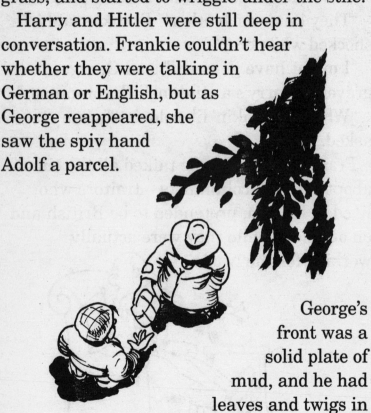

George's front was a solid plate of mud, and he had leaves and twigs in

his hair, but he looked very smug indeed.
"That should slow him down!" he grinned.
"What did you do?"
"I let his tyres down!"

5

Hitler and the spiv talked for a couple more minutes in low voices, then separated. The children ducked down. They heard Harry walk away. A few moments later a car started up. Harry drove everywhere. Petrol was rationed, but Harry could always get it. Frankie and George heard the car pull into the road and head away in the direction of the village.

Seconds later, they heard a rustle in the hedge as Hitler picked up his bike. They heard the rubbery truckle of the flat rear tyre as he moved off, and the low curse as the Führer noticed it. Satisfied, George moved down the slope under the bridge and motioned to the other two to follow.

"I thought we were going to ambush him!"
Frankie said, but George explained Plan B.
The water was shallow under the Bridge,
and there were stepping stones. They'd cross
the river that way and catch the Führer just
as he reached the village. "That way, once
we've nobbled him, we can get help quickly."
It probably wasn't the best plan of the war,
but it was certainly the best plan George
had cooked up that day.

It's not easy finding stepping-stones in the
mist, but they managed. After that it was

just a question of getting across the fields as quickly as possible. As they tramped through the damp grass, Frankie told George about the parcel she'd seen exchanged.

"Money, probably. English money, for the invasion," said George.

The church tower stood, a dark misty silhouette against the sky, and they made their way towards it.

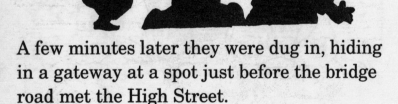

A few minutes later they were dug in, hiding in a gateway at a spot just before the bridge road met the High Street.

"I'm tired," Sam complained. "And my socks is wet!"

George sneered. "Here we are," he said, "about to win the war, and all this kid can do is moan. Hiter'll be here any minute. All we have to do is wait."

And that's what they did. They waited.

And waited.

And waited.

"What's happened?" asked George after a while. "He should have been here by now."

"Maybe he's realised we're on to him, and gone home," Frankie suggested.

"Don't be daft," George retorted. "After coming all this way?"

"How far is it from Berlin?"

"Well . . . I'm not sure. But it's a long way on a bike!"

They heard a noise. Several noises. The clickety-clickety-click of a bike, the crunch of boots on the road, and the heavy breathing of somebody who is puffed out. George grinned.

"No wonder he's been a while," he whispered. "He's had to walk it!"

As he spoke, they saw Hitler come trudging round a bend in the road. His hat was perched back on his head and he looked even more bad-tempered than he looked on the newsreels.

Frankie turned to her little brother. "OK, Sammy," she whispered. "You know the plan? As soon as we jump him, you run straight to the police station and tell them what we told you to say."

"That we've caught Hitteler, and they've to come right away!" said Sam, proud to have remembered such a long speech.

"Maybe you're not so daft after all," George said.

CLICKETY CLICKETY CLICKETY

Hitler was really close now. Only a few yards away.

. . . A few feet . . .

CLICKETY CLICKETY CLICKETY CLICK

George held up a hand. "Wait for the signal ... wait ... wait ..." Frankie's heart was pounding.

CHARGE!

6

After invading Poland and Czechoslovakia, Hitler must have been getting over-confident. He certainly seemed surprised when the gang flew like howling spitfires out of the gate next to him.

It crossed Frankie's mind that George was a bit *too* much like a spitfire, sticking his arms out wide and going:

NYYYAAAAAAAOOOoWWW.!!

RAT-TAT-TAT-TAT-TAT !!

RAT-TAT-TAT-TAT-TAT-TAT-

TAT-TAT-TAT-

TAT-TAT !!!

but it seemed to do the trick, and before Hitler knew where he was, where he was was on the floor, bowled over like a Nazi nine-pin by the three members of the Evacuee Squadron.

One other thing about Hitler. His English

was a whole lot better than Frankie had expected. In fact he swore quite fluently until George gagged him with his own scarf. He'd jumped on Hitler, losing his glasses in the process, and now he was all over the great dictator like a rash. His legs were wrapped round the Führer's throat, and he seemed to be trying to unscrew his head.

Frankie was so fascinated that she momentarily forgot the plan, until George nodded towards Sam and gasped, "Why is . . . he . . . still here!?" Frankie pulled herself together and sent her little brother racing off to the police station.

There was a bit more struggling. "Get his bag!" yelled George. Frankie ran over and grabbed the duffle bag. She up-ended it, and emptied the contents on to the road. Then as George struggled to control the thrashing, growling Nazi chief, Frankie put the bag over the Führer's head, and pulled the cord tight. She vaguely noticed black smudges on her fingers. Perhaps it was oil from the bicycle chain . . . ?

Hitler was still trying to say something, but it was all muffled by the scarf and the duffle bag. "Get his gun!" George said. But

when Frankie walked over to the little pile
of stuff from the bag, she discovered that
the gun wasn't a gun after all.

"It's a walking stick," she said, handing it
to George.

There was other stuff lying in the road:

A flattened
bowler hat,

a pair of tatty
old shoes,

and that paper
packet that Adolf
had got from the
traitor Harry.

George was talking to his captive. "Brought disguises, did you Mein Herr? Thought you could sneak into Blighty, did you? Well you . . . can . . . think . . . again!" Each word was punctuated with a clonk from the walking stick and a muffled yelp from inside the duffle bag.

A clatter of hobnails announced the arrival of the police. George was disappointed to see that they had only sent one lowly constable to arrest such a big cog in the war machine.

Still, maybe the sergeant was busy phoning

Mr Churchill with the good news?

"Don't forget!" he said firmly as he gave up his prisoner, "we caught him, we get the reward!" He ignored the funny look the constable gave him.

The little procession made its way along the high street. Frankie walked in front pushing the bike. Behind her the constable led Hitler – now handcuffed but still with

the bag over his head. Bringing up the rear, carrying Hitler's little bundle of disguises, was George. His glasses were bent, but he didn't care. He had just done his bit for his country.

 He thought maybe the excitement was making him hallucinate, because as they passed the grocers he could have sworn he saw Laurel and Hardy walking out of the door . . .

News travels fast in a small village, especially when it's broadcast by a four-year-old. Suddenly about twenty evacuees appeared and fell into step behind George. They'd all turned out to support the home team.

Frankie dropped back and pointed to the paper parcel the constable was carrying. She could see a little tear where he'd looked inside. "What is it?" she asked. "We thought it must be money. You know, to keep his War Machine going."

"It's not money, my love," the constable

said with a funny little smile. "It's something far more interestin' than that!"

Frankie didn't understand that, but she staggered on with the bike.

As they neared the police station, Frankie heard someone call her name. It was Mrs Tanner. At least, it was someone who looked like Mrs Tanner. Except that Mrs Tanner didn't usually walk around with a mixing bowl and wooden spoon, or wear a lace-trimmed lampshade on her head, or have a big home-made spider bouncing around on wire.

"Frances Crabtree!" the woman shrieked. "What in the blue blazes are you doing? If you've been arrested, I'll—"

"We haven't been nicked, Mrs T," Frankie sang back. "We've just caught Hitler!"

"Caught *Hitler*?" Mrs Tanner looked perplexed.

"Where are you going Mrs T?" Frankie asked, (she nearly added "Looking that silly!").

Mrs Tanner stopped being cross. Instead, she began to glow and preen.

"Do you like it?" she asked, giving Frankie a twirl. "I'm Little Miss Muffet!"

"Are you?"

"For the dance tonight. It's fancy dress."

"Oh. *Right*!"

Sam was sitting on a chair eating a sandwich when they arrived at the station, his feet swinging several inches off the ground.

"Did you see Laurel and Hardy?" he asked. Frankie didn't have time to reply because the desk sergeant was already talking to the constable.

"So we've caught Adolf at last, have we?"

"Yes, Sarge," the constable replied with a smirk.

There was a burst of protest from the duffle bag. The constable passed the paper parcel over the desk and watched as the sergeant looked inside. "Well, well," he said quietly.

"The kids say they saw him get it from Harry!" the constable said.

"Really?" The sergeant turned and boomed into the back office, "Davies!" A large dragon head appeared through the hatch. Frankie jumped. So did the sergeant.

"Davies," he said crossly, "Get that stupid thing off your head, replace it with your regulation helmet and fetch Harry Seymour out of the Rose and Crown!

And tell all those kids outside they can clear off home!"

"But Sarge," The dragon protested in a muffled voice, "I was just going off duty. I'm taking me missis to the fancy dress dance. She's Saint George.

"I don't care if she's Saint Pancras Station, lad. Get a move on!"

The dragon removed its head to reveal a red-faced constable, who promptly disappeared through the back door. The sergeant lifted the desk flap, and stepped through to join the arresting party.

"I've always wanted to see Hitler, face to face," he said.

And with that, he whipped off the duffle bag.

7

Frankie and George looked at each other in horror. Sam sat and chomped absent-mindedly on his sandwich. "Well, well, well," the sergeant said. Standing before them, purple with rage, was Wet Blanket, the town clerk.

Two nasty lumps were already coming up on his forehead, and his boot-polish moustache was a grubby smear all over his sweaty face.

"I want to bring charges!" he fumed, rubbing his head. "These little brats assaulted me!"

Frankie and George shrank under his glare. He may not have been the Great Dictator, but he still scared the pants off them.

"Look at me!" he ranted. "My clothes are ruined. And so is my bicycle!"

"And where were you going, sir, if I may ask?"

"I was on my way to the fancy dress dance!" Mr Watts-Blunkett snapped.

"As Adolf Hitler?" the constable exclaimed. "That's poor taste, that is!"

Mr Watts-Blunkett turned a withering eye on him. "Not as Adolf Hitler, you moron!" he bellowed, looking more like Hitler than ever. "As Charles Chaplin, the film star!"

"Ah," the constable nodded. "That would explain the hat." He held up the bowler, now flattened where George had sat on it in the struggle.

"Something wrong, Mr Watts-Blunkett?" the sergeant asked. The clerk was staring at the bowler. He had gone deathly pale.

"Th . . . that hat . . ." he said in a flat, horrified voice. "It belongs to the mayor. It's his best hat. I . . . I only borrowed it for this evening. He'll be livid!" He swung round and pointed at George. "You!" he snarled. "You destructive little thing. You're going to regret this night as long as you live!"

"He may not be the only one." It was the sergeant who spoke. As Mr Watts-Blunkett turned to demand to know what he meant by that remark, his eyes fell on the paper parcel in the sergeant's hand. Wet Blanket's mouth snapped shut.

The parcel was open now, and the children could finally see what was in it. Not money, but the biggest piece of black-market meat any of them had seen for a long, long time.

"Well, Mr Watts-Blunkett?"

"I've never seen that meat before in my life!"

"That's not true!" George protested. "We were there, and we saw Harry give that parcel to Hitl— to Wet Bl— to *him*, at the crossroads by the bridge!"

Watts-Blunkett's face which had only just regained its normal colour, now started to go red all over again.

"Right, you kids," said the sergeant, "you'd best go on home."

"But they attacked me!" spluttered the

clerk.

The door opened and Constable Davies came in with Harry. Harry did not look happy. He looked even less happy when he saw the pack of meat in the sergeant's hand. His eyes darted shiftily round the room, and ended up on Mr Watts-Blunkett. The clerk was clearly wrestling with his conscience.

"It was him!" he burst out suddenly, pointing at Harry. "He practically forced me to buy the stuff. I've never bought anything on the black market before!"

"Oh yeah!" Harry sneered. "What about that petrol last week? And those American nylons your missis wears?"

The clerk looked as if he might explode. He turned to the sergeant. "I'll co-operate, Sergeant, I – I know where he keeps the stuff!"

Harry went off like a roman candle. "You shut your trap!" he yelled.

"He's got it in a barn on one of the farms," Wet Blanket blurted out. "I can take you there if you like . . . only please *please* keep my name out of this . . ."

The last thing the children saw as they left the station was the sergeant laughing his head off.

"I've got you this time, Harry, boy" he was saying. "Indeed I have!"

"Well, we didn't get a reward!" George

sighed, as they got outside.

"And we didn't catch Hitler *or* win the war," grumbled Frankie.

"But at least Horrible Harry got his just desserts!" George grinned.

"And I got a Spam sandwich!" cried Sam, to which there was no answer.

They walked through the village. Loads of people were about now, making their way to the village hall dance, all wearing the ingenious fancy dress they'd cobbled together from scraps. George saw Laurel and Hardy again, though this time it was obviously the grocer and his wife.

The dragon clattered past them, still in its uniform shoes. "Evening Constable Davies," Frankie said. The dragon was so surprised that it nearly fell on its tail.

As they passed the village hall they could
hear the party in full swing. "What about
scrumpin' tomorrow?" George suggested.

Frankie shook her head. "I don't think so, George," she said, clutching Sam's hand. "This war might last for weeks yet. We might need things like that to live on. I mean, suppose Adolf Hitler really does come? What then?"

George walked along in silence, thinking.

"Well," he said, finally. "If Adolf really does come, he'll just have to get his own apples, won't he?"

THE CRABTREE CHRONICLES

0 340 69989 2 Book 1: Let's Get Caesar!   £3.50 ❐
0 340 69966 3 Book 2: Blame it on the Bard!   £3.50 ❐
0 340 69991 4 Book 4: The Diddle of the Sphinx £3.50 ❐

All Hodder Children's books are available at your local bookshop, or can be ordered direct from the publisher. Just tick the titles you would like and complete the details below. Prices and availability are subject to change without prior notice.

Please enclose a cheque or postal order made payable to *Bookpoint Ltd*, and send to: Hodder Children's Books, 39 Milton Park, Abingdon, OXON OX14 4TD, UK.
Email Address: orders@bookpoint.co.uk

If you would prefer to pay by credit card, our call centre team would be delighted to take your order by telephone. Our direct line *01235 400414* (lines open 9.00 am–6.00 pm Monday to Saturday, 24 hour message answering service). Alternatively you can send a fax on *01235 400454*.

TITLE		FIRST NAME		SURNAME	

ADDRESS	
DAYTIME TEL:		POST CODE	

If you would prefer to pay by credit card, please complete:
Please debit my Visa/Access/Diner's Card/American Express (delete as applicable) card no:

Signature .... Expiry Date: ....

If you would NOT like to receive further information on our products please tick the box. ❐